Date: 2/21/18

J 796.334 REA
Stewart, Mark,
Real Madrid C.F. /

PALM BEACH COUNTY
LIBRARY SYSTEM
3650 SUMMIT BLVD.
WEST PALM BEACH, FL 33406

First Touch Soccer

Real Madrid C.F.

By
Mark Stewart

Norwood House Press
Chicago, Illinois

P.O. Box 316598 • Chicago, Illinois 60631
For more information about Norwood House Press please visit our website at
www.norwoodhousepress.com or call 866-565-2900.

Photography and Collectibles:
The trading cards and other memorabilia assembled in the background for this book's cover and interior pages
are all part of the author's collection and are reproduced for educational and artistic purposes.

All photos courtesy of Associated Press except the following individual photos and artifacts (page numbers):
Editions Rencontre SA (6), Monopol Sportphotos (10 top), Longacre Press Ltd. (10 bottom),
Author's Collection (11 top), Topps, Inc. (11 middle), Panini America Inc. (11 bottom),
Victor Cup (16), Rafo/Mostar (23).

Cover image: Paul White/Associated Press

Designer: Ron Jaffe
Series Editor: Mike Kennedy
Content Consultants: Michael Jacobsen and Jonathan Wentworth-Ping
Project Management: Black Book Partners, LLC
Editorial Production: Lisa Walsh

LIBRARY OF CONGRESS CATALOGING-IN-PUBLICATION DATA
Names: Stewart, Mark, 1960 July 7- author.
Title: Real Madrid C.F. / By Mark Stewart.
Description: Chicago Illinois : Norwood House Press, 2017. | Series: First
  Touch Soccer | Includes bibliographical references and index. | Audience:
  Age 5-8. | Audience: K to Grade 3.
Identifiers: LCCN 2016058206 (print) | LCCN 2017005793 (ebook) | ISBN
  9781599538624 (library edition : alk. paper) | ISBN 9781684040810 (eBook)
Subjects: LCSH: Real Madrid Club de Futbol--History--Juvenile literature.
Classification: LCC GV943.6.R35 S84 2017 (print) | LCC GV943.6.R35 (ebook) |
  DDC 796.334/64094641--dc23
LC record available at https://lccn.loc.gov/2016058206

© 2018 by Norwood House Press. All rights reserved.
No part of this book may be reproduced without written permission from the publisher.

This publication is intended for educational purposes and is not affiliated with any team, league, or association
including: Real Madrid Club de Futbol, Liga de Futbol Profesional, The Union of European Football Associations
(UEFA), or the Federation Internationale de Football Association (FIFA).

302N--072017
Manufactured in the United States of America in North Mankato, Minnesota.

Contents

Meet Real Madrid C.F. ... 5
Time Machine ... 6
Best Seat in the House ... 9
Collector's Corner ... 10
Worthy Opponents ... 12
Club Ways ... 14
On the Map ... 16
Kit and Crest ... 19
We Won! ... 20
For the Record ... 22
Soccer Words ... 24
Index ... 24
About the Author ... 24

Words in **bold type** are defined on page 24.

In soccer, star players often go by a one-word nickname. In this book, we use the nickname followed by the player's (*full name*).

James Rodriguez and Lucas Vazquez rush toward Cristiano Ronaldo after a goal. Real Madrid is one of the best teams in La Liga, Spain's top soccer league.

Meet Real Madrid C.F.

The city of Madrid is the capital of Spain. Soccer has been popular there for more than 100 years. Madrid is home to the Real Madrid Club de Futbol, which is Spanish for Royal Madrid Football Club. In Spain, when people say "futbol" they are talking about soccer, not American football.

Real Madrid fans have had a lot to cheer about over the years. The club has been champion of the Spanish League more than 30 times.

Time Machine

In 1902, the Madrid Club de Futbol was formed. In 1920, King Alfonso of Spain gave the club the title of "Royal" and it became known as Real Madrid. During the 1950s and 1960s, Real Madrid was one of the best clubs in the world. That is still true more than 50 years later. The club's great players include **Ferenc Puskas**, Emilio Butragueno, and Raul (*Raul Gonzalez Blanco*).

Raul turns an eye-level ball into a spectacular goal during a 2001 match.

Real Madrid fans work together to display a banner showing their support of the players.

Best Seat in the House

Real Madrid plays its home games in Santiago Bernabeu Stadium. It is named after a beloved player and team president. The stadium opened in 1947. It has been enlarged many times since then. Now it holds more than 85,000 fans. In 1982, the final match of the **World Cup** was played in the stadium.

Collector's Corner

These collectibles show some of the best Real Madrid players ever.

Ricardo Zamora
Goalkeeper
1930–1936
Zamora was a tough man in the rough game of the 1930s. Spain's award for best keeper is now named after him.

Francisco Gento
Forward
1953–1971
Gento's lovely passes from the left wing set up hundreds of goals. He was a great goal scorer himself.

ZINEDINE ZIDANE

Midfielder
2001–2006
Zidane was always on the attack. His goal in the 2002 **Champions League** final is one of the best ever.

CRISTIANO RONALDO

Forward
First Year with Club: 2009
It only took a couple of seasons before Real Madrid fans were calling Ronaldo the team's greatest player. He was an unstoppable scorer.

GARETH BALE

Midfielder/Forward
First Year with Club: 2013
Few soccer players have ever had the speed and power of Bale. He is equally good on either side of the field.

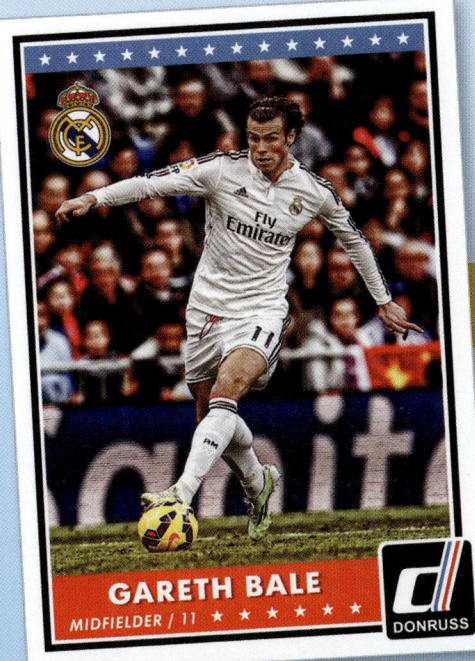

Worthy Opponents

Real Madrid's main rival is Barcelona. The two cities are rivals in Spain and so are their soccer clubs. Madrid is also home to the soccer club Atletico Madrid. Their matches with Real Madrid draw big, noisy crowds. In the years when Barcelona struggled, Atletico gave Real Madrid all it could handle.

Pepe (*Kepler Laveran Lima Ferreira*) drives toward the goal during a 2014 match against Barcelona.

Club Ways

Soccer fans can be very superstitious. That is one of the reasons why Real Madrid fans fell in love with Cristiano Ronaldo. Ronaldo had to be the last player off the bus. He would not leave the locker room until he touched the game ball. He always stepped on the field with his right foot first. And during halftime, he changed his hairstyle.

Real Madrid fans loved Cristiano Ronaldo's different hairstyles. They also love that he averaged a goal a game for the club!

ON THE MAP

Real Madrid brings together players from many countries. These are some of the best:

1. **Gareth Bale** • Cardiff, Wales
2. **Raymond Kopa** • Noeux-les-Mines, France
3. **Fabio Cannavaro** • Naples, Italy
4. **Luis Figo** • Almada, Portugal
5. **Ferenc Puskas** • Budapest, Hungary
6. **Hugo Sanchez** • Mexico City, Mexico
7. **James Rodriguez** • Cucata, Colombia
8. **Alfredo Di Stefano** • Buenos Aires, Argentina

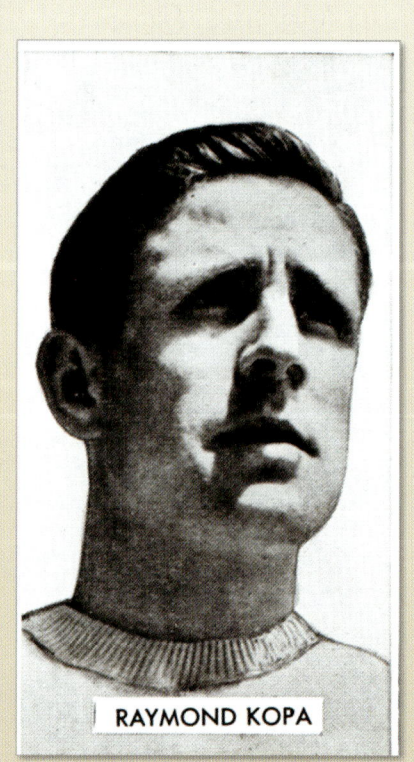

RAYMOND KOPA

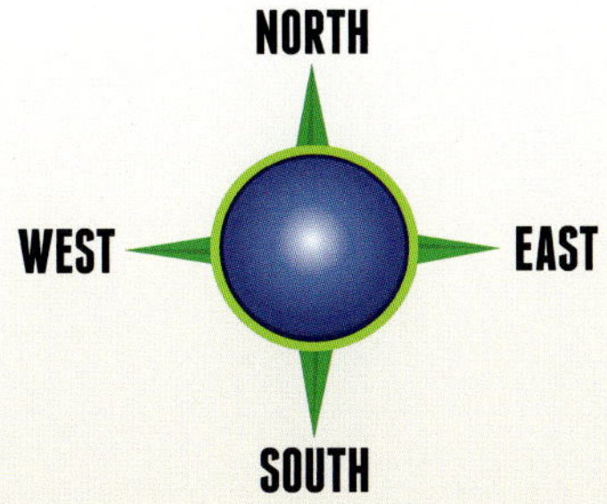

Map of Europe

Real Madrid's home stadium is in Madrid, Spain.

World Map

17

The crown atop Real Madrid's club crest is easy to see on Toni Kroos's uniform.

Kit and Crest

When Real Madrid players get their uniforms dirty, everyone knows it. They wear white from head to toe for home matches. Their away kit is usually dark blue or purple. The club's crest has changed little since the 1940s. The letters MCF stand for Madrid Club de Futbol. The crest has a purple band and a red crown.

We Won!

From 1955 to 1960, no club in the world could equal Real Madrid. The team starred Alfredo Di Stefano, Francisco Gento, Raymond Kopa, Ferenc Puskas, and Hector Rial. Real Madrid won the **European Cup** five years in a row. The European Cup became the Champions League in the 1990s. Real Madrid has won the tournament more than 10 times.

Alfredo Di Stefano – in white – starts to celebrate as his shot skips past the goalkeeper during the 1960 European Cup final.

For the Record

Real Madrid has won more than 60 major championships!

European Cup/Champions League

1955–56
1956–57
1957–58
1958–59
1959–60
1965–66
1997–98
1999–00
2001–02
2013–14
2015–16

Club World Cup

2014

Copa del Rey*

19 championships (from 1905 to 2014)

Super Cup

2002
2014
2016

Intercontinental Cup

1960
1998
2002

*Copa del Rey means King's Cup in Spanish. It is the championship tournament held each year in Spain.

These stars have won major awards while playing for Real Madrid:

1957   Alfredo Di Stefano • European Footballer of the Year
1958   Raymond Kopa • European Footballer of the Year
1959   Alfredo Di Stefano • European Footballer of the Year
2001   Luis Figo • World Player of the Year
2002   Ronaldo (*Ronaldo Luis Nazario de Lima*) World Player of the Year
2002   Ronaldo • European Footballer of the Year
2003   Zinedine Zidane • World Player of the Year
2006   Fabio Cannavaro • European Footballer of the Year
2006   Fabio Cannavaro • World Player of the Year
2008   **Iker Casillas** • Goalkeeper of the Year
2009   Iker Casillas • Goalkeeper of the Year
2010   Iker Casillas • Goalkeeper of the Year
2011   Iker Casillas • Goalkeeper of the Year
2012   Iker Casillas • Goalkeeper of the Year
2013   Cristiano Ronaldo • Golden Ball
2014   Cristiano Ronaldo • Golden Ball

IKER CASILLAS

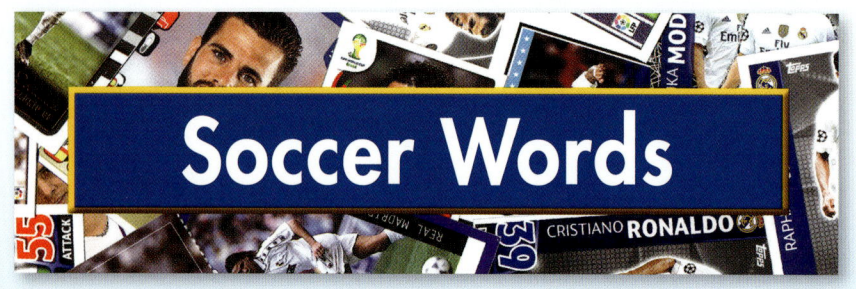

Soccer Words

Champions League
A competition between the best clubs in Europe.

European Cup
A club championship tournament that began in 1955. It became the Champions League in 1992.

World Cup
The championship of soccer. Teams of all nations compete in this tournament every four years.

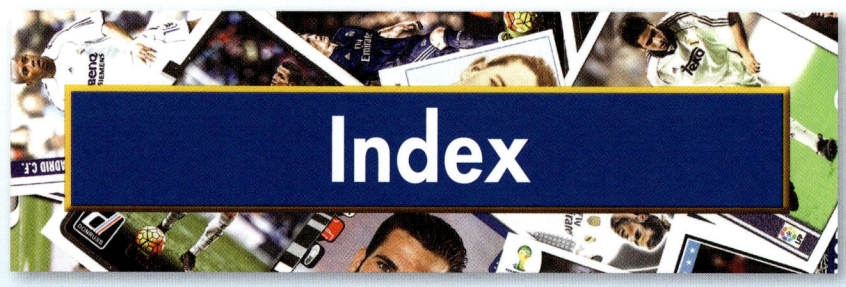

Bale, Gareth	11, **11**, 16
Bernabeu, Santiago	9
Butragueno, Emilio	6
Cannavaro, Fabio	16, 23
Casillas, Iker	23, **23**
Di Stefano, Alfredo	16, 20, **21**, 23
Figo, Luis	16, 23
Gento, Francisco	10, **10**, 20
King Alfonso of Spain	6
Kopa, Raymond	16, **16**, 20, 23
Kroos, Toni	**18**
Pepe	**13**
Puskas, Ferenc	6, **6**, 16, 20
Raul	6, 7
Rial, Hector	20
Rodriguez, James	**4**, 16
Ronaldo	23
Ronaldo, Cristiano	**4**, 11, **11**, 14, **15**, 23
Sanchez, Hugo	16
Vazquez, Lucas	**4**
Zamora, Ricardo	10, **10**
Zidane, Zinedine	11, **11**, 23

Photos are on **BOLD** numbered pages.

About the Author

Mark Stewart has been writing about world soccer since the 1990s, including *Soccer: A History of the World's Most Popular Game.* In 2005, he co-authored Major League Soccer's 10-year anniversary book.

About Real Madrid C.F.

Learn more at these websites:
www.realmadrid.com/en
www.fifa.com
www.teamspiritextras.com